The Tiara Club

at Emerald Castle

For Princess Fiona, and all her friends
at Sandham Middle School
VF

With very special thanks to JD

www.tiaraclub.co.uk

ORCHARD BOOKS
338 Euston Road, London NW1 3BH
Orchard Books Australia
Level 17/207 Kent St, Sydney, NSW 2000

A Paperback Original
First published in 2008 by Orchard Books

Text © Vivian French 2008
Cover illustration © Sarah Gibb 2008
Inside illustrations © Orchard Books 2008

The right of Vivian French to be identified as the author of this
work has been asserted by her in accordance with the
Copyright, Designs and Patents Act, 1988.

A CIP catalogue record for this book is available
from the British Library.

ISBN 978 1 84616 870 3

3 5 7 9 10 8 6 4 2

Printed in Great Britain
The paper and board used in this paperback are natural recyclable
products made from wood grown in sustainable forests.
The manufacturing processes conform to the environmental
regulations of the country of origin.

Orchard Books is a division of Hachette Children's Books,
an Hachette Livre UK company.

www.hachettelivre.co.uk

The Tiara Club

at Emerald Castle

Princess Leah

and the Golden Seahorse

By Vivian French

ORCHARD BOOKS

The Royal Palace Academy
for the Preparation of Perfect Princesses

(Known to our students as "*The Princess Academy*")

OUR SCHOOL MOTTO:
*A Perfect Princess always thinks of others
before herself, and is kind, caring and truthful.*

Emerald Castle offers a complete education for Tiara Club princesses while taking full advantage of our seaside situation. The curriculum includes:

A visit to Emerald Sea World Aquarium and Education Pool	*Swimming lessons (safely supervised at all times)*
A visit to Seabird Island	*Whale watching*

Our headteacher, Queen Gwendoline, is present at all times, and students are well looked after by the school Fairy Godmother, Fairy Angora.

Our resident staff and visiting experts include:

QUEEN MOLLY (Sports and games)	*KING JONATHAN (Captain of the Royal Yacht)*
LORD HENRY (Natural History)	*QUEEN MOTHER MATILDA (Etiquette, Posture and Flower Arranging)*

We award tiara points to encourage our Tiara Club princesses towards the next level. All princesses who win enough points at Emerald Castle will be presented with their Emerald Sashes and attend a celebration ball.

Emerald Sash Tiara Club princesses are invited to return to Diamond Turrets, our superb residence for Perfect Princesses, where they may continue their education at a higher level.

PLEASE NOTE:
Princesses are expected to arrive at
the Academy with a *minimum* of:

TWENTY BALLGOWNS
(with all necessary hoops,
petticoats, etc)

TWELVE DAY DRESSES

SEVEN GOWNS
suitable for garden parties,
and other special
day occasions

TWELVE TIARAS

DANCING SHOES
five pairs

VELVET SLIPPERS
three pairs

RIDING BOOTS
two pairs

Swimming costumes,
playsuits, parasols, sun hats
and other essential outdoor
accessories as required

Hello - and do you like the seaside?
I absolutely LOVE it - which is why I'm
VERY happy Emerald Castle is by the sea.
I'm so lucky to be here - especially as
you've come to keep me company. And
Amelia, Ruby, Millie, Rachel and Zoe are
here too - we're the Daffodil Room
princesses. Oh! Did I tell you who I am?
I'm Princess Leah! How do you do?

Chapter One

When we first got to Emerald Castle I thought our headteacher, Queen Gwendoline, was horribly fierce, but luckily I was wrong. She can be stern, but it's only because she wants us to be totally PERFECT princesses. Most of the time she's very smiley, and she thinks up a new project for us practically every single day. We weren't at all surprised when she came marching in while we were eating our breakfast to tell us about yet another idea.

"Good morning, princesses!" she said cheerfully. "I've got SUCH a lovely outing planned for you! Fairy Angora is going to take

you to Emerald Sea World. It's a wonderful place; you'll walk down and down a long dark passage until you're actually UNDERNEATH Emerald Bay, and then you'll come to a room with a glass ceiling – and you'll see all kinds of beautiful fish swimming above you!"

The horrible twins, Diamonde and Gruella, were sitting at the table next to ours, and I heard Diamonde whisper, "BORING!"

Luckily our headteacher didn't hear her, and she went on, "There's an aquarium as well, with an education pool that has a wonderful golden seahorse in it – one of the very few golden seahorses in the world! Of course," and for a second Queen Gwendoline looked ferocious, "you will NOT touch the seahorse." She smiled again. "And I have another surprise. A group from the Princes' Academy have been studying marine life, and they've very kindly agreed to show you the creatures in the education pool. I want to thank them, so I thought we might end the day with a party here at Emerald Castle."

Of course that made us all sit BOLT upright. Queen Gwendoline laughed when she saw our shining eyes. "I can see you think that's a good idea! But please work hard today; at the end of your visit there'll be a test, and I want you all to do well. Ten tiara points will be given to any princess who gets full marks, together with an invitation to sit at the top table at the party tonight. But now, if you'll excuse me, I must hurry off and consult Fairy G about decorations."

As Queen Gwendoline strode away Millie sighed happily. "At last! A party!" she said. "I've got this beautiful new dress, and I thought I'd NEVER be able to wear it."

"Me too," Ruby agreed.

"Huh!" Diamonde sneered from behind us. "We've got DOZENS of new dresses, haven't we, Gruella?"

Gruella nodded.

"So NONE of you will look as pretty as we do." Diamonde put down her cup with a crash. "The princes will be queuing up to ask us to dance! Come on, Gruella. Let's go and choose what we're going to wear." And she grabbed her sister and zoomed towards the dormitories.

"Diamonde! Gruella!" Fairy Angora looked MOST surprised. "What ARE you doing? Please go back to your places, and listen to my instructions."

I thought for a moment that Diamonde and Gruella were going to refuse, but they didn't.

Our assistant fairy godmother is very kind and sweet most of the time, but she can get cross – and when she does she gives LOADS of minus tiara points. The twins sighed heavily, and stomped back to their seats.

Chapter Two

Half an hour later we were walking along a grassy path on the top of the cliffs. Diamonde and Gruella nearly had a fit when they heard we were WALKING to Emerald Sea World, but Fairy Angora told them it would only take five minutes, and it wasn't worth going by coach.

"Mummy says Perfect Princesses NEVER walk on grass," said Diamonde loudly.

"That's right," Gruella agreed. "Grass is for ORDINARY people."

Zoe began to giggle, and the twins glared at her. "What's so funny?" Diamonde demanded.

"It just sounded so silly," Zoe said. "And what do you mean, ordinary people?"

Gruella looked at Diamonde. "YOU tell her, Diamonde."

"She means people who aren't SPECIAL, like us." Diamonde stuck her nose in the air.

I hate it when the twins talk like that. It always makes me want to do the exact opposite of what they say, and sometimes I SO don't think about what I'm doing.

"I must be VERY ordinary, then," I said. "I love grassy spaces. You can't do cartwheels on marble floors." And as Diamonde and Gruella stared, I gave a hop and a skip and turned a cartwheel.

At once Fairy Angora came hurrying up to me. "My precious petal," she said, and I could see she was trying not to laugh. "I DON'T think Queen Gwendoline would think that was QUITE the right way for a Perfect Princess to behave...although you did do it beautifully."

I hung my head, and pushed my glasses back up my nose. "I'm very sorry, Fairy Angora." And then, because it was true, I added, "I'm afraid I was showing off."

"That's right!" Diamonde chipped in. "And that just PROVES she's not special like me and Gruella! We're PERFECT princesses!"

Fairy Angora shook her head. "I'm afraid a Perfect Princess never boasts, Diamonde. On the other hand, they DO always tell the truth, and confess when they've done something wrong. That's two minus tiara points for you, Diamonde, but only one for Leah. And now let's hurry – Emerald Sea World is just around the corner!"

I thought Diamonde was going to explode. As Fairy Angora

floated on ahead of us she hissed, "Just you WAIT, Little Miss Show-off! I'll make you REALLY sorry!" And she gave me the meanest glare.

I was about to snap back, but luckily Ruby had overheard Diamonde. She tucked my arm in hers, and whisked me away. "Look!" she said cheerfully. "There's the entrance! It looks wonderful – and I just can't wait to see the golden seahorse. My cousin saw it when she was at Emerald Castle, and she said it's just darling!"

Chapter Three

Emerald Sea World was fabulous. We walked down a long, narrow passage lit by glowing lamps, then suddenly it was light again – and over our heads was the glass ceiling! We were actually under the sea! It was SO magical. The glass was a ceiling to us, but for the fish it was a floor, and we could see them really clearly as they swam peacefully to and fro. We stood and gazed, while Fairy Angora told us all about them.

I particularly liked the angel

fish, but when I got out my sketch book and pencils and began drawing Diamonde jogged my elbow as she walked past. My picture was ruined, so I turned

over the page to start again. I'd almost finished when I noticed she was standing beside me.

"Ooops-a-daisy!" she said, and pretended to slip – knocking all my colouring pencils onto the ground. "Oh – SILLY me!" She gave me a totally false smile. "DO let me help you pick them

up, Leah!" She grabbed at the pencils, and as she handed them back I saw that all the points were broken.

"What a shame!" Diamonde looked horribly pleased with herself. "You really should be more careful, Leah. You won't be able to show off your drawing now!" And she hurried off.

I couldn't believe she'd been so mean! But the very next minute Fairy Angora asked us to make our way to the aquarium, and I had to put my pencils in my bag and follow my friends... I was feeling SO angry. But then

Millie stopped to wait for me, and she whispered, "Don't take any notice of Diamonde! She's only cross because she got minus tiara points. You can borrow my pencils later, if you like." And I felt a hundred times better. Aren't friends just WONDERFUL?

We could hear a lot of talking as we followed the signs for the aquarium, and as Fairy Angora opened the door we saw a group of princes standing round a pretty little pool. At once Diamonde and Gruella patted their hair, and together they minced up to the oldest prince, who was up to his elbows in water.

"You're SO brave!" Diamonde breathed, and her eyes looked very wide and admiring. "Aren't you scared you'll be bitten by a crab?"

The prince didn't look at all

impressed. "Crabs don't bite," he said. "They pinch." He took one of the empty glass jars from the shelf by the pool, and scooped up a little red crab. Then he held it out to Diamonde.

"YUCK!" she screamed, and backed away.

"It can't hurt you," the prince told her. He caught my eye, and he must have seen that I was smiling because he held the crab in my direction. "Do you want to hold it?"

"OK." I took the jar as gently as I could. The crab waved its pincers, but it didn't seem unhappy, and I studied it carefully.

"I'd never noticed they have four pairs of legs before," I said.

The prince looked pleased. "Actually it's five pairs of legs,

but the fifth pair develop into pincers, and they don't use them for walking. I'm Prince Rosso, by the way."

"I'm Princess Leah." I handed back the jar, and Prince Rosso tipped the little crab onto a stone at the edge of the pool. It scuttled sideways, and plopped into the water. "Is the golden seahorse in here?"

Rosso grinned. "Can't you see her?"

Chapter Four

I leant over the pool, and stared into the blue-green water. My friends came to look as well, and Diamonde and Gruella pushed their way to the front...but we couldn't see anything that looked golden. There was plenty of green seaweed, several lovely pink anemones waving their frond-like fingers, and lots of tiny silver fish darting about – but then I saw something glitter, and I gasped. "She's TINY!"

And she was. I don't know what I'd expected, but the golden seahorse was about as big as my little finger, and SO beautiful.

She came swimming out of a tiny grotto made of shells that was half hidden by the seaweed, and for a moment or two she looked as if she was dancing in the water.

"Poor little thing." Prince Rosso sounded sad. "She dances in case there's another golden seahorse out there...but she's all on her own."

"She must be very lonely," Rachel sighed.

Diamonde put on her most superior expression. "It's only a fish," she said. "How can you feel sorry for a fish?"

Millie tweaked my glasses off, and balanced them on the end of her nose. "'A Perfect Princess treats all animals, be they large or small, with courtesy and consideration,'" she quoted, and she sounded EXACTLY like Queen Gwendoline!

Diamonde and Gruella were the only ones who didn't laugh. They were watching the little seahorse, and Gruella suddenly

asked, "Is she made of real gold?"

"'Fraid not, old bean." One of the other princes moved forward, and smiled toothily at the twins. "Although she is TERRIBLY valuable. Really special. Worth an absolute FORTUNE."

"REALLY?" Diamonde gave him a strange look.

"My ma and pa tried to buy her for me, but the jolly old people here said no." The prince made a weird neighing noise, and I realised he was laughing. "Bit of a shock for the aged parents, I can tell you! 'Sorry, Wincey old boy,' they said, 'but no little seahorse for you!' So they bought me a pony instead. Little LAND horse – get the joke? Haw! Haw! Haw!"

I could see Zoe and Amelia were trying not to giggle, and Ruby, Millie and Rachel were hiding smiles as they stared into the pool. Fairy Angora gave a little cough.

"Thank you, Prince Wincey," she said politely. "A splendid joke.

But now it's time to make your way to the Sea Life classroom, my precious petals. Hurry along, now – you'll find it just at the end of the corridor."

Prince Wincey gave a sweeping bow as we walked away, but Prince Rosso just nodded. "We've

got to go back to school now," he said. "I expect we'll see you later."

I couldn't help hoping he was right!

Ruby and Amelia were ahead of me as we got to the classroom door, and I heard them gasp as they walked in. A moment later I saw why; Queen Gwendoline herself was sitting behind the teacher's desk.

"Welcome, princesses," she said. "I hope you've enjoyed your time here. It's one of my favourite places, and I never fail to be enchanted by the education pool.

Now, shall we see how much you have learnt from your visit?"

Of course I felt nervous as we sat down; I always do when it comes to tests, but I needn't have worried. The questions were easy, and all of us in Daffodil Room scribbled away as Queen Gwendoline read out each of the questions. The final question was, "How many legs does a crab have?" and Ruby gave me the teeniest wink as we happily wrote down the answer.

Then, as Charlotte from Rose Room went round collecting our papers, Diamonde put up her hand. "Please excuse me, Your Majesty," she said in a very wobbly voice, "but I don't feel well."

Queen Gwendoline looked at her over her spectacles. "You'd better go and find Fairy Angora. Princess Leah, will you go with

Princess Diamonde, please?"

"But I want Gruella to come with me!" Diamonde sounded annoyed. Queen Gwendoline raised her eyebrows at this, and Diamonde quickly added, "PLEASE, Your Majesty."

"Very well," Queen Gwendoline said. "Princess Gruella, you may go too."

Chapter Five

It was SO obvious Diamonde didn't want me to come with her and Gruella. As soon as we were outside the classroom she gave me a huge false smile. "It's OK, Leah. Really. Gruella will look after me, won't you, Gruella?"

Gruella nodded.

"Well, I don't know..." I said.

"If you're sure..."

"I'm QUITE sure," Diamonde said firmly. "You go back to the classroom!" and then she seized her sister's hand and dashed off in the direction of the education pool.

I was left staring after them. It didn't look to me as if Diamonde was ill. It looked as if she was up to something! And it may not have been very princessy of me, but I REALLY wanted to know what it was.

I hurried along the corridor after the twins, and when I got to the door at the end I opened it just a little way, and peeped

through...and there was Diamonde
fishing about in the water, while
Gruella stood beside her holding
a glass jar and looking anxious.

"Hurry up, Diamonde!" she whispered, and at that exact moment Diamonde dropped something shiny and golden into the jar – and I ZOOMED into the room.

"What on earth are you DOING?' I gasped. "That's the golden seahorse!"

"But I want it!" Diamonde glared at me. "I want Mummy to buy it for ME!" She grabbed the glass jar, and tucked it into her bag. "I'm BORED of puppies and ponies! I want a golden seahorse because it's SPECIAL!"

"What is it that's so special, Diamonde dear?"

As Diamonde and Gruella jumped guiltily, I saw Fairy Angora standing behind me. She doesn't ever mean to sneak up on us, but she does move VERY quietly.

Diamonde let out a loud moan. "Queen Gwendoline sent me to find you, Fairy Angora. I feel VERY sick..."

"You poor darling," Fairy Angora said, and she put her hand on Diamonde's forehead. "You do feel rather feverish. Come with me, and we'll find you somewhere to lie down."

"Can Gruella come with me?"

Diamonde whispered. "I want her to hold my hand."

"Of course," Fairy Angora smiled. "Leah, petal – you'd better go back to the classroom."

As Diamonde moved away, leaning heavily on Fairy Angora's arm, my mind was racing. She was holding her bag very tightly, and I was really worried about the golden seahorse. I knew it would be dreadful if I told Fairy Angora what Diamonde had done, but I had to do something – and then I had an idea.

"Please, Fairy Angora," I said, "Diamonde's bag looks SO heavy. Why don't I take it back to the classroom for her?"

I saw Diamonde's eyes flash, but Fairy Angora looked pleased. "That's a very kind thought,

Leah. Here you are—"

She put out her hand to take the
bag, but Diamonde clutched it
closely to her chest. "Gruella can
carry it!" she squealed. "Leah
can't have it!"

"But Diamonde," Fairy Angora protested, "Leah's only trying to help you."

"No she isn't!" Gruella grabbed one of the bag's handles. "Let ME take it—"

CRASH!

The bag opened, and the glass jar fell onto the floor and smashed. Diamonde and Gruella screamed, and Fairy Angora gasped as water splashed everywhere – and I dived to save the poor little golden seahorse as she lay quivering on the cold stone floor.

"I'm so sorry," I whispered as I scooped her up in my cupped hands. "I really am," and I dropped her back in the pool. She sank to the sandy bottom, and my heart leapt into my mouth – but then she gave a wriggle, and swam unsteadily into her grotto.

"Quick!" I turned to Fairy Angora. "PLEASE help the little seahorse – she must have had a dreadful shock!"

Fairy Angora gave me a comforting smile, and waved her wand over the pool. Tiny stars floated down, and danced on the surface of the water – and there was the golden seahorse dancing underneath!

"I think," Fairy Angora said, "she'll be quite all right."

"Thank you SO VERY much!" I breathed.

Fairy Angora patted my shoulder. "It's because you popped her back in the pool so quickly. You did very well, my little darling."

"Princess Leah has done extremely well," said Queen Gwendoline's voice from the doorway. "But I would very much like to know what Princesses Diamonde and Gruella thought THEY were doing?"

Chapter Six

You know I said Queen Gwendoline could be very stern? Well, Diamonde and Gruella were positively shaking in their shoes as they followed our headteacher away. And it may sound weird, but I really did feel a little bit sorry for them.

Fairy Angora gave us our test

results, and we'd all done well – but Daffodil Room had top marks, and ten tiara points each! We were SO excited, and we were even more excited when Fairy Angora told us we'd be sitting at the top table with the princes.

"We'd better hurry back to Emerald Castle, my precious petals," she said, "so you can get ready for the party!"

And that's just what we did. It was such fun putting on our best party dresses, and we twirled round and round in Daffodil Room admiring each other.

"Maybe Prince Rosso will ask you to dance!" Rachel teased me.

"Or maybe it'll be Prince Wincey!" Amelia sank down into a glorious curtsey. "Thank you SO much, dear prince!"

Millie pretended to bow. "Hi,

old bean! Hope you're sooper dooper! Haw! Haw! Haw!"

She sounded so exactly like Prince Wincey that Zoe and Ruby collapsed in giggles, and we were all smiling as we made our way down the stairs.

The Emerald Castle ballroom looked absolutely wonderful; Fairy G had decorated it with sea-green ribbons and swathes of silver net hung with tiny silver bells, and on the ceiling glitter balls flashed sparkles of blue-green light.

"It looks as if we're underwater!"

Millie whispered as we made our way to the top table.

"Hey!" Rachel winked at me. "Here come the princes – don't they look grand?"

Rachel was right. The princes came striding in behind King Ferdinand, and they looked so different I suddenly felt shy.

I looked down at my plate, and I told myself how silly I'd been to think a prince as handsome as Prince Rosso would EVER ask me to dance.

"Princess Leah?"

I looked up – and there he was beside me, bowing.

"Erm...hello," I said, and I sounded SO unprincessy!

And then there was a fanfare of trumpets, and I saw that everyone was looking at us. I blushed BRIGHT red, and Prince Rosso bowed again.

"Princess Leah," he said, "I have been asked to present you with this small gift, on behalf of Emerald Sea World," and he handed me a small parcel. I took it, and my hands were trembling as I opened the box.

It was the sweetest little golden seahorse necklace!

"THANK YOU!" I did my best to curtsey, but I wobbled dreadfully. "It's BEAUTIFUL!"

"Hurrah for Princess Leah!" Zoe called, and everyone began to

clap...and I blushed even more.

Prince Rosso waited while I put the necklace on, and then he smiled. "Would you like to dance?" he asked.

That night as we got ready for bed, Rachel heaved a huge sigh. "Hasn't today been completely and utterly amazing?"

She was right. We'd all danced non-stop, and even Prince Wincey had turned out to be good fun.

As we snuggled under our bedclothes we blew each other goodnight kisses...and I blew an extra one – just for you!

Don't miss  website at:

www.tiaraclub.co.uk

Keep up to date with the latest
Tiara Club books and meet all
your favourite princesses!

There is SO much to see and do,
including games and activities. You can
even become an exclusive member of the
Tiara Club Princess Academy.

PLUS, there's an exciting
 Emerald Castle competition
with a truly AMAZING prize!

Be a Perfect Princess – check it out today!

What happens next?
Find out in

Princess Ruby
and the Enchanted Whale

*Are you good at singing? I'm not.
If I'm honest, even frogs hop away and
hide under their lily pads when I sing.
But Perfect Princesses are supposed to
be able to sing like nightingales – at
least, that's what Queen Mother Matilda
says. Ooops – I'm so sorry! I haven't
introduced myself. I'm Princess Ruby.
Have you met the other princesses from
Daffodil Room? Amelia, Leah, Millie,
Rachel and Zoe? They're like me. VERY
pleased you're here with us!*

"La la la LAH! La la la LAH! La la la la la la LAH!"

I could see Queen Mother Matilda was turning purple, but what could I do?

"Princess Ruby!" she snapped. "You are NOT trying! Take three minus tiara points, and make sure you do better next lesson!" Then she gathered up her music sheets and swept away from the piano and out of the music room. I sighed, and Millie patted my shoulder.

"Never mind, Ruby," she said. "I think you've got a lovely voice. It's just...different."

Diamonde was standing beside me, and she nudged her twin sister. "Perfect Princesses ALWAYS sing in tune, don't they, Gruella?"

"That's what Mummy says," Gruella agreed.

"So anyone who doesn't sing in tune can't EVER be a Perfect Princess!" Diamonde said smugly, and she gave me SUCH a superior look.

Amelia made a face as the twins skipped out of the music room hand in hand. "Why do they always have to be so horrid?" she asked.

Zoe looked wise. "I think it's

their mother's fault," she said. "My dad met her once, and she never stopped talking about the twins and how totally perfect they were. He said he actually felt sorry for them, because he could tell they were completely spoiled."

"That's right," Leah nodded. "And because there are two of them they can stick together, and they don't mind what anyone else thinks."

Rachel sighed. "It's still very annoying, though."

~◯ Want to read more? ◯~
Princess Ruby and the Enchanted Whale
is out now!